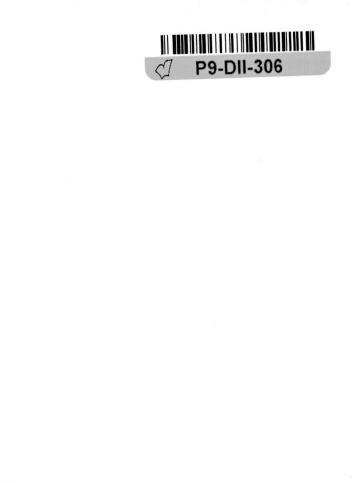

CHICKIE RIDDLES

by Katy Hall and Lisa Eisenberg

pictures by Thor Wickstrom

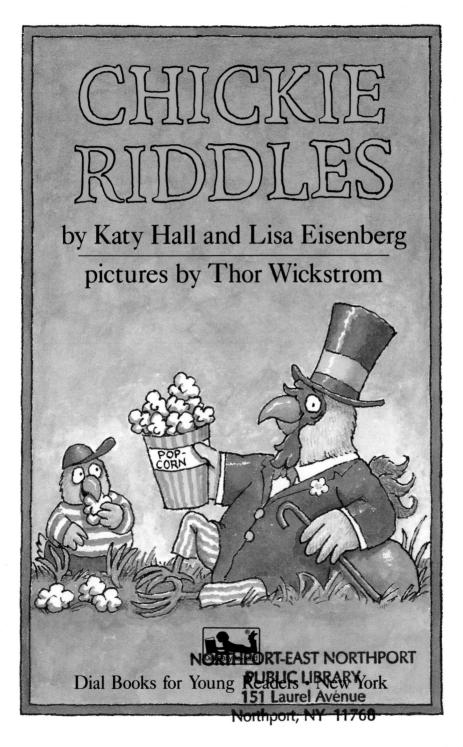

Dial Books for Young Readers • New York

Published by Dial Books for Young Readers
A Division of Penguin Books USA Inc.
375 Hudson Street
New York, New York 10014

Text copyright © 1997 by Katy Hall and Lisa Eisenberg
Pictures copyright © 1997 by Thor Wickstrom
All rights reserved
Printed in Hong Kong
The Dial Easy-to-Read logo is a registered trademark of
Dial Books for Young Readers,
a division of Penguin Books USA Inc.,
® TM 1,162,718.

Library of Congress Cataloging in Publication Data
Hall, Katy.
Chickie riddles / by Katy Hall and Lisa Eisenberg ;
pictures by Thor Wickstrom.
p. cm.
ISBN 0-8037-1778-4.—ISBN 0-8037-1779-2 (library)
1. Riddles, Juvenile. 2. Chickens—Juvenile humor.
[1. Chickens—Wit and humor. 2. Riddles. 3. Jokes.]
I. Eisenberg, Lisa. II. Wickstrom, Thor, ill. III. Title.
PN6371.5.H3476 1997 818′.5402—dc20 94-33170 CIP AC

First Edition
1 3 5 7 9 10 8 6 4 2

The full-color artwork was prepared using pen and ink,
colored pencils, watercolor, and gouache.

Reading Level 2.0

Dedicated to
Chicken Little and Henny Penny

K.H. and L.E.

To Sylvie and Sosha

T.W.

What is Snow White's
brother's name?

Egg White—get the yolk?

If you crossed a cocker
spaniel, a French poodle, and
a rooster, what would you get?

A cockerpoodledoo!

What looks just like half a chicken?

The other half.

Where do hens come from?

Hennessee.

Where do chicks come from?

Chickago.

Why did the farmer hire the chicks to fix up the coop?

They were *cheep* workers.

Which side of a chicken
has the most feathers?

The outside.

Why did the chicken
cross the road?

To get to the other side.

Why did the chicken go
halfway across the road?

She wanted to lay it on the line.

What do you get if you cross
a road with a chicken?

To the other side.

Why did the turkey cross the road?

To show he wasn't chicken.

Why do hens lay eggs?

Because if they dropped them,
they'd break.

Where do chickens
go to dance?

To the Fowl Ball.

How do hens and roosters dance?

Chick to chick.

Can a chicken really be worth $2,000?

Only if she saves all her money.

What kind of weather do chickens like best?

Fowl weather.

What holiday do roosters love?

Feather's Day!

Why do chickens think
cooks are mean?

They beat eggs.

What game do baby chicks
love to play?

Peck-a-boo!

When is dinner
in the henhouse?

At eggs-actly seven o'clock.

What's made of chicken and
noodles and can leap tall
buildings in a single bound?

Chicken Soup-erman!

What's Chicken Soup-erman's real name?

Cluck Kent.

What day do chickens
hate most?

Fryday.

What do you have to know
to teach a chicken tricks?

More than the chicken.

What do chickens say
when they want
to trade nests?

"Let's make an eggs-change!"

Why did the hen take
a hot bath?

She wanted to lay a hard-boiled egg!

Why did the hen stop laying eggs?

She was tired of working
for chicken feed!

What do you call a chicken
that likes to clean?

A feather duster.

What do you get if you cross
a dog and a chicken?

A pooched egg!

What do you get
if you cross a chicken
and a police officer?

A hen that really lays down the law!

Have you heard the joke
about chicken pox?

Shhh! Don't tell it!
It might spread!

What's the opposite
of cock-a-doodle-do?

Cock-a-doodle-don't!

Why didn't the chicken look both ways before she crossed the road?

She was a dumb cluck!

Why did the dinosaur
cross the road?

There weren't any chickens
back then!

How many chickens can you
put into an empty coop?

Just one. After that it isn't empty!

Why should you never
tell a joke to an egg?

Because it might crack up!

Why did the chicken run
away?

She felt cooped up!

Why did the hen run away from the mall?

She heard it was a chopping center!

Why did the farmer invite
his two new chickens
to a party?

He was trying to make
both hens meet!

How do we know
a rooster loves his comb?

Because he'll never part with it!

What's the favorite game in the henhouse?

Chickers.

What kind of jokes
do chickens like best?

Corny ones!

$12.99

DATE			

MAR 1997